Pookins
Gets Her Way

Helen Lester
Illustrated by Lynn Munsinger

Houghton Mifflin Harcourt
Boston   New York

For more information about the importance of being considerate and to download a free audio version of this story, visit

www.hmhbooks.com/freedownloads

Access code: beconsiderate

Text copyright © 1987 by Helen Lester
Illustrations copyright © 1987 by Lynn Munsinger

www.hmhco.com

Library of Congress Cataloging-in-Publication data is on file.

ISBN 978-0-544-32406-0
Manufactured in China
SCP 10 9 8 7 6 5 4 3 2 1
4500503826

Pookins was used to getting her own way.

If Pookins did not get her own way
she would make faces,

throw apples,

and yell very loudly.

And because nobody wanted her to
make faces, throw apples, and yell very
loudly, Pookins always got her own way.

She had ice cream for breakfast.

She never ate her vegetables.

She did not pick up her clothes, and
she got all the toys she ever asked for.

She roller-skated in the living room.

And she went to bed very late,
sometimes even after the owls.

One day Pookins went out for a skip.
She wore the party dress she was supposed
to save for parties — just because she felt like it.
Before long she met a magic gnome.

He asked, "What can I do for you?"
"Lots," said Pookins.

"I want three wishes. First I want a
new pair of cowboy boots, or else I'll make
faces, throw apples, and yell very loudly."

The gnome rubbed his magic hat
and Pookins got her cowboy boots.

"Now," demanded Pookins, "I want a beautiful queen hat. Make sure it has plenty of diamonds, or else I'll make faces, throw apples, and yell very loudly."

Pookins got her queen hat—with plenty of diamonds.

"And finally," she said, "I want to become a
flower, the prettiest flower in the world."
The magic gnome looked at Pookins and asked,
"Are you sure you want to become a flower?"
"If you don't let me become a flower," warned
Pookins, "I'll make faces, I'll throw . . ."
"Never mind," said the gnome.

"Becoming a flower is not easy," said the gnome.
"First we must put you in a pot."

"Then you need some nice soil around your roots."
He dumped a load of dirt all over Pookins's lovely
new cowboy boots.

"And of course you will need plenty of water."
The gnome gave Pookins a good watering all over.
Soon the soil felt very squishy in the pot.

"Finally," chirped the gnome, "you must stand
in the sun for hours and hours and hours."
And with that he rubbed his magic hat.

There stood Pookins.
In the sun.
In a pot.
Very wet.
Up to her ruffles in soil.

Hours and hours and hours
and even more hours passed.

Pookins was a flower.

By this time Pookins decided that getting
her own way wasn't so much fun after all.
"Let me out of this pot," she cried, "or else —"
"Or else what?" said the gnome.

"Flowers can't throw apples or yell loudly, and I
can hardly see your face through all those petals.
You wanted your own way and I gave it to you."
Pookins felt very sorry for herself and began to cry.

Suddenly without warning it began to rain.
"My hat, my magic hat," cried the gnome.
"It will shrink and I will lose my powers."
For the first time Pookins felt sorry for the gnome.
"Get under my petals. I'll keep you dry," she said.

The gnome stayed there until the rain stopped. "Pookins," he said, "you helped me so I will help you, on one condition. You must put all of your bad faces, loud yells, and apples into my magic hat forever. Then I will let you out of the pot."

Pookins quickly agreed.

The magic gnome then rubbed his hat and
Pookins was no longer a flower.

The happy Pookins skipped quickly home.
And she only kept one small apple — just in case.